Catch a snowflake
from the sky...

sparkle
sparkle
wish

Spread our snowy
angel wings...

flutter

flutter

swish

Sing a cheery
Christmas song...

jingle jingle hum

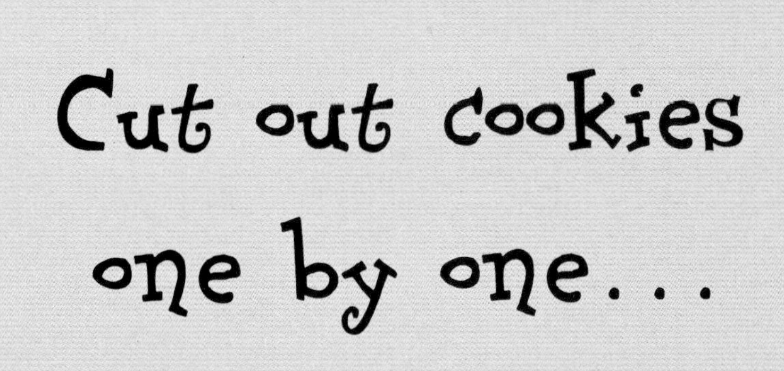
Cut out cookies
one by one...

sprinkle

sprinkle

yum

Reach to hang an ornament...

shiny
shiny
bright

Place a golden
star on top . . .

twinkle
twinkle
night

Share a
favourite Christmas
book . . .

cuddle cuddle snug

Hang the stockings,
time for bed . . .

kisses kisses hug

Wake at dawn
and jump for joy...

bouncy
bouncy
leaps

Hand in hand,
we run and see...

Merry Christmas,
little
cheeps!